FIND YOUR WAY TO

Muppet

TREASURE ISLAND™

FIND YOUR WAY TO
Muppet
TREASURE ISLAND™

By Kate McMullan

Illustrations by Michael K. Frith

Adapted (loosely) from the movie Muppet Treasure Island
Original screenplay by Jerry Juhl & Kirk R. Thatcher and James V. Hart
Based (very, very loosely) on the novel by Robert Louis Stevenson

MUPPET PRESS
MAMMOTH • LONDON

First published in Great Britain in 1996 by Mammoth
an imprint of Reed Children's Books
Michelin House, 81 Fulham Road, London SW3 6RB
and Auckland, Melbourne, Singapore and Toronto
Reprinted 1996
Cover design by Graphiti Design & Production
Illustrations by Michael K. Frith on facing page and
pages 4,6,12,21,25,28,34,35,43,45,51,53

ISBN 0 7497 2784 5

Printed and bound in Great Britain
by Cox & Wyman Ltd, Reading, Berkshire

START BY READING THIS

Are you ready to take a trip to *Muppet Treasure Island*?
Are you ready to have some wild adventures? To sail on
a ship with a pirate crew? To seek buried treasure? To be
led by a captain who happens to be a frog?

If you are, then begin reading on page 1. Keep reading
until you come to a page where you are asked to make a
choice. Decide what you want to do, and then turn to
that page. Keep reading and making choices until you
come to THE END. Now one adventure is over. But there
are plenty of others in this book. Go back to where you
started. A new adventure is always about to begin!

Tomorrow's Saturday—your birthday!

"There's only one thing I want this year," you tell your mom and dad. "A set of drums."

You just know you're cut out to be a drummer with a really hot rock band. All you need to get started are the drums. And a pair of drumsticks. Not to mention some tight black jeans and a torn T-shirt. But, hey...one thing at a time.

"I don't think so," says your mom. "Drums are *much* too noisy."

"Drums are uncivilized," adds your dad.

"But...but...but...," you sputter.

"Besides," your mom cuts in, "we've already bought you your gift. And are *you* going to be surprised!"

"Oh, yeah?" you say.

Cool! Last year your mom and dad bought you a watch for your birthday. It has glow-in-the-dark stars and comets that move around on its face. And a guaranteed-to-last-a-year battery.

Maybe this year they got you a new skateboard. Or a pair of in-line skates. Or a new computer game. Or maybe even a new computer!

Go to page 2.

You wake up the next morning expecting something great! You run down to breakfast. In honor of your birthday, your dad has made his super–healthy multi–grain waffles. Your mom has stuck a candle right in the middle of yours.

"Happy birthday to you!" they sing.

After you blow out the candle, they point to your present.

You stare at the small rectangular package. It has fuzzy blue kittens on the wrapping paper. It's tied with a bright red bow. Definitely not a skateboard. Or a computer. The best you can hope for at this point is a computer game. You pick it up. Too heavy for a game. What can it be?

Go to page 3.

"Why don't you open it?" suggests your mom.

You rip off the ribbon, tear off the kitten paper.

"Oh, look," you say. "A book." You try to sound excited. "It...uh, looks good," you add.

It also looks *old*. What's with your parents, anyway? Couldn't they even have bought you a new book?

"It's *Treasure Island*," says your father. "It was a favorite of mine when I was a boy."

"It's a limited edition," adds your mom. "The bookseller told us that makes it very valuable."

"We thought it was just the thing to start you off on becoming a book collector," your dad tells you.

"Thanks," you manage to say. "Thanks a lot."

If you want to start reading *Treasure Island* right away, turn to page 8.

If you want to dig into that multi-grain waffle first, turn to page 15.

"Are you kidding?" you say. You shut *Treasure Island*. You go to your desk and open your math book, *Problems So Hard They Might Actually Kill You*. Ugh! So many little numerals and signs and squiggly lines.

Uh–uh. No way are you doing math problems. Not on your birthday. So back you go to *Treasure Island*. This time you open it in the middle. You check out a picture that looks like...Fozzie Bear! Huh? What's he doing in *Treasure Island*? And why the ship in the bottle?

Wait a second. Are you losing your marbles? Or can you hear the Fozzie guy talking? "This is a model of daddy's biggest boat," he says. "What I need is a friend to go on a voyage with me, Mr. Bimbo!"

And bingo! You're there! Standing by Fozzie!

Go to page 10.

"Put vous stinky heads on altar!" shouts the boar king.

You try to obey. But you can't bend over.

"You there!" he shouts. "More bend over!"

"I–I can't," you manage.

"All right!" shouts Gonzo. "Defy the boars!"

"There's something in the way," you explain.

"Guards!" cries the king.

The boar guards rush over to you. They pull you to your feet. One guard sticks his hand into your sweatshirt pocket and pulls out...Fluffy!

"Squee!" squeaks the little guinea pig as the boar guard holds him up for all to see.

A hush falls on the clearing. Without a word, the guards untie everybody. Then they fall to their knees.

"Uh, what's going on?" you ask.

The boar holding your guinea pig points to the stone altar. Now you recognize the primitive fat beast painted on it. It's Fluffy!

"Vous bring us sacred animal," the boar king explains. "Now we worship BOOM-A-FLUFF-A and *vous*!"

"Well, okay," you say agreeably. And even though it *is* something of a sacrifice, you live the rest of your life on that island, worshiped as a god.

THE END

"I might make a pretty good pirate," you begin. "But I was wondering, um, just where *are* we?"

Long John throws his head back. He laughs long and loud. "That's a good one, eh, Polly?" he says at last. "Wants to know where we are!" Long John puts his face close to yours. "We're on Treasure Island," he whispers. "And if any of the loot is going into your pockets, we'd better make *you* a pirate!"

Suddenly a hairy little guy rushes up to you. He's wearing a top hat that's full of holes. He doesn't exactly look like a pirate—except that he's waving a pair of cutlasses.

"Yes, Mad Monty?" says Long John. "What is it?"

Go to page 7.

"The initiation!" Monty shouts in your face.

P–ew! You're pretty sure *his* initiation didn't involve brushing his teeth.

The next thing you know, the pirates are lining up. Monty is wrapping a filthy bandanna around your eyes. You can't see a thing. Monty pushes you forward. You stumble. Ow! Something whacks you on the rear end! Ooh! Something bops you on the head! The pirates are shoving you on down the line.

"Have a bit of grog!" someone shouts, dousing you with the foamy drink.

"Keep going!" you hear Long John cry. "It's almost over now!"

At last you come to the end of the line. You stumble in the sand. Somebody rips off your blindfold. Long John is smiling down at you.

"You made it!" he exclaims. "You and Jim both!"

Now you notice the boy sitting by you in the sand.

"Meet Jim Hawkins," Long John says.

Jim nods in greeting. He doesn't look very happy.

"Now let's kill 'em!" suggests Monty. He puts one cutlass to Jim's throat and one to yours. "Together!"

Go to page 54.

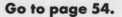

"May I be excused, please?" you ask.

"But you haven't touched your waffle," says your dad.

"I can't eat now," you say. "I'm too eager to start reading this book." You hold up *Treasure Island*.

"Well, go on then." Your dad chuckles. He turns to your mom. "What did I tell you, honey?" you hear him say as you head for your room. "It was the perfect present!"

You trudge upstairs. Perfect present, your foot. This is turning out to be the worst birthday of your life. No drums. No cake. Just that lousy waffle.

But, hey. It's only eight o'clock in the morning. Maybe something exciting will happen yet.

Go to page 9.

You flop down on your bed. You know your mom won't bend her "no TV before seven in the evening" rule—even on your birthday. So you might as well do a little reading.

You open *Treasure Island*. The old book smells funny. The pages are yellowish brown. You check out an illustration of some people in old-fashioned clothes. They're sitting around a table. Some of them look like pirates. But yuck! You shut the book. No way can you read something that smells like a dead fish.

You reach over to your bedside table. You pick up your all-time favorite book, *Muppets Forever!* You can't count the number of times you've read it. But that's the trouble. You know every page by heart.

You've got both books in your lap. Which one's it gonna be?

If you pick *Muppets Forever!*, turn to page 24.

If you pick *Treasure Island*, turn to page 32.

"Whoa! How did I *get* here?" you ask.

"Mr. Bimbo brought you," says Fozzie.

You look around. Whoever Mr. Bimbo is, you figure he's zapped you back in time about 200 years.

"Mr. Bimbo lives in my pointer finger," Fozzie explains. "Maybe he brought you here from the moon."

"Just play along with him," someone whispers.

You look around. "Rizzo?" you say.

"In the fur," says the rat.

Then you see Gonzo, and a boy about your age.

"See," begins Gonzo, "me and Rizzo and Jim Hawkins here, we're talking to young Squire Trelawney..."

"Young, rich, half-witted Squire Trelawney," puts in Rizzo.

"That's me," agrees Fozzie happily.

"We're talking to him about hiring a ship," Jim says.

"To hunt for treasure," Gonzo adds. "With this map!" He points to a map spread out on a table.

"*Shh*," cautions Jim. "Remember, pirates are looking for this map."

Gonzo grins. "And they want to kill us for it!"

"Come on," says the young squire. "Let's go down to the harbor and sail away in one of daddy's boats!"

Go to page 45.

The harder Pew squeezes your arm, the harder you grit your teeth. Just when you think you can't grit any harder, a musket fires into the room. Then pirates are everywhere! They're crashing through doors! They're bashing in windows.

"We want that treasure map!" cries one pirate. "It's ours by rights! Give it up, Bones!"

"Come on!" Jim Hawkins grabs your arm. He pulls you out the door and down the back stairs. Somehow you make it out of the inn. Gonzo and Rizzo are right on your heels. The four of you run up the road.

You duck under a bridge as it begins to rain. No one breathes as Pew leads his gang of cutthroats over the bridge. They're still carrying on about that map. At last they're out of sight.

"Oh, boy," says Rizzo. "That was a close one!"

"I still don't get it," Gonzo says. "What map do those pirates want, anyway?"

You reach into your sweatshirt pocket. You pull out a dogeared map. "I think it's this one," you say.

"Hey, where'd you get that?" asks Rizzo.

"Billy Bones slipped it to me," you tell them. "Just before he...died."

Go to page 25.

What a pessimist! Sure, these are bloodthirsty pirates who'd make their own mothers walk the plank for a chance to get rich quick. *Sure* they have guns and muskets and pistols and razor-sharp swords. But there's one thing they're a bit short on.

Can you guess what it is?

Take a moment to study the typical pirate pictured below. What quality is he most obviously missing?

A. taste in trousers
B. taste in hairstyles
C. taste in footwear
D. a working brain

**If you picked answers A, B, or C,
turn to pages 34–35,
study the pirate crew again,
then take the test over.**

If you picked D, turn to page 33.

"I heard every word you said!" you shout at the evil trio. "And I'm telling Captain Smollett!"

"Think again," says Polly.

"And after you think," says Monty, "I kill you!"

"Not so fast," says a voice behind you.

What is it around here with these voices? You're getting a stiff neck from whipping your head around.

But, hey, it's Long John! You're saved!

"Get 'em, Long John!" you cry. "Get 'em!"

Long John raises his eyebrows. "I'm with them, mate. I just didn't want Monty to have all the fun."

Monty and Long John strike out at you with their swords. You dodge, feeling a breeze from their blades!

"Captain!" you cry. "Captain Smollett!"

"Hush, dear," says a voice behind you.

You whip your head around. No one's there.

"Here we are," says another voice.

You look up. "Mom?" you say. "Dad?"

"You sure were into that book," Dad says. "Take a break and open your *other* birthday present now." He points to the corner of your room, where all tied up with a red ribbon is a big, fancy set of drums.

"Shiver me timbers!" you cry. "Rock band, here I come!"

THE END

Long John helps you ashore. Since your hands are tied, he holds the map in front of your eyes. You read it, and the three of you tramp through the jungle. At last, you reach a cave. It's filled with treasure!

Long John's eyes glitter. "Flint's treasure," he breathes. "And it's all mine!" He draws his sword.

"No, *mine!*" yells Monty. He whips out his sword, and the two of them begin battling over the treasure.

"Cease!" shouts a lady pig from the mouth of the cave. She's holding a coconut in each hand. *Hi–yaaa!* She heaves the coconuts at Monty and Long John, knocking them senseless.

The pig saunters over and unties you. *"Bonsoir, mon ami!"* she says. "I'm Benjamina Gunn. I'm worshiped as a goddess around here. It's not bad, except that the nightlife's a little lame. I'm thinking of starting a band. I don't suppose you play the drums or anything?"

After a few practice jams, you, Benjamina, and some of the more musical boars on the island are ready for prime time. You name the band "Low Down Dirty Pirates," and you become a mega success!

THE END

"How's that waffle?" your dad asks.

"*Mmmm*," you reply as you deftly hide a big chunk of it in your napkin. Yecch! It tastes like hay. But Mom and Dad are chewing away. They don't seem to notice.

"Um, may I please be excused?" you ask as soon as the rest of your waffle is safely hidden in your lap.

"Sure," says your mom. "I'll bet you want to get started on your book!"

"Right," you say.

Your mom smiles. "That bookseller promised you'd get a kick out of the story," she says. "A big kick!"

"Right," you say again.

Stuffing your waffle-filled napkin under one arm and *Treasure Island* under the other, you run upstairs. You dump most of your waffle in the trash. Then you go over to your pet guinea pig's cage. "Here, Fluffy," you say, tossing in a chunk of waffle. "Want a little treat?"

Fluffy sniffs the thing. Then he looks up at you. His eyes seem to say, *Are you kidding?*

Go to page 17.

You don't go through that wide-open kitchen door, but as Pew bumbles around the room, *he* does. He keeps on going. Billy runs and slams the door behind him.

"Whew!" You all breathe a sigh of relief.

But before you calm down too much, the voice of Mrs. Bluveridge, the innkeeper, bellows from...somewhere.

"*DISHES!*" she shouts. "*WASH THOSE DISHES!*"

Gonzo scratches his head. "How does she *do* that?"

"I'm outta here, mates," says Billy Bones. "I do grub. I do grog. But I *don't* do dishes!" He staggers out the door.

"I'll wash," you volunteer.

"I'll dry," Jim says.

"I'll break!" says Rizzo, smashing a plate on the floor.

"I'll watch," Gonzo offers.

The four...er, make that *three* of you work for hours. But you don't make much progress on that stack of dishes. Your stomach's growling. Your fingertips have turned to raisins. But you keep going, hoping that someday, this dishwashing job will come to ...

THE END

"Yeah," you tell Fluffy. "I know what you mean."

You take Fluffy out of his cage. You let him run around on your bed while you stare at your new book—well, your *old* book.

The cover has a pirate on it. He's a totally mean–looking, one–legged dude with a crutch. On his shoulder stands his parrot. But...wait a second. That's not a parrot. That's a lobster!

Just as Fluffy crawls inside the front pocket of your sweatshirt, you open the book right to the middle. There's that pirate again. But, hey! What's happening? He's *moving!* He's drawing back his crutch and...BAM!

Go to page 18.

Ow! That pirate kicked you! Right between the eyes! Your head is whirling. Your eyes are spinning. Your ears are ringing—with your mom's voice: *That bookseller promised you'd get a kick out of the story!*

For a minute, all you can see are stars. Thousands of them. Millions, even. You look around. You're not in your bedroom anymore. You're on a beach. It's dark out—except for the big bonfire that's burning over by the dunes.

Now you hear drums—and music. You look around. Hey, it's Dr. Teeth and his band!

"What's going on?" you mutter.

"Let's go see, shall we?" says a deep voice.

You turn. There at your side is the pirate! The one with the missing leg. The one with the lobster.

"Don't dawdle," warns the pirate. He puts an arm around your shoulder and begins pulling you toward the bonfire. All around it are other pirates. They're dancing and drinking and waving their cutlasses.

"Sorry about the boot to your noggin," the pirate says as you approach the fire. "By the way, I'm Long John Silver, at your humble service."

"Oh," you mutter. "Hi, Mr. Silver."

Go to page 19.

"It's 'Long John' to me friends," says the pirate with a smile. You think he looks friendly—sort of.

Suddenly the lobster on his shoulder gives out an earsplitting "Squawk! Polly want a cracker!"

"Here's Polly, saying 'hello,'" says Long John.

"*Polly?*" you say. "But that's a lobster."

"Aye," says Long John. He seems to think it's the most natural thing in the world to be walking around with a big, orange lobster perched on his shoulder. "And a fine crustacean he is, too," he adds.

You check Polly out. He has a patch over one eye. The other eye is checking *you* out. Polly doesn't look all that friendly.

You and Long John stop by the bonfire. You're so close you can feel the heat of its flames. "Ah, pirates at play," says Long John. Then he leans forward and whispers in your ear, "Now tell ol' Long John the truth. Deep down in that heart of yours, haven't you always wanted to become a pirate?"

If becoming a pirate has never even crossed your mind, turn to page 36.

If you've always thought it might be cool to be a pirate, turn to page 6.

What you think of is—RUN!

Off you go! You're running faster than you've ever run before. You keep going, and going, and going. You run through a patch of jungle. You run onto a strip of beach. You drop to the sand, panting for air. You glance behind you. No sign of those pirates.

You've almost caught your breath when you hear a scraping noise. Then, in the moonlight, you make out the shape of a small boat landing on the beach.

You see the silhouettes of three passengers. Whoever they are, they're awfully quiet. Are they pirates? Smugglers? Cutthroats? And, most important, are you going to stick around to find out?

If *yes,* turn to page 37.

If *not a chance,* turn to page 28.

"...nine hundred eighty-four...," you count.

"Are we there yet?" whimpers a goat-faced pirate. "My feet hurt! Plus, I have to go to the bathroom."

"Stop whining, Clueless!" cries Long John as you count out the last two baby steps. "Look! The skeleton tree! We dig here!"

Dangling above your head are three hideous skeletons, twisting and turning in the breeze.

"Oh!" cries Clueless. "This place is curse–ted!"

Clueless is half–crazy with fear. His other half is *totally* crazy, so he's not much help with the digging. Long John hands the shovel to you.

"Wake me when you hit pay dirt," he says. Then he finds himself a shady patch and settles in for a nap.

Go to page 22.

You start digging. It's hot, sweaty, backbreaking work. But you keep at it. After several hours, you've dug yourself a crater the size of a Buick. But you don't see any treasure.

You need a break. Long John is snoring away, so you climb out of the pit. You lean up against a wall of vines. Yikes! What you thought was a solid wall wasn't. You tumble backward, landing on your backside.

You look around. You've fallen into the mouth of a cave. All around you are tiki god statues and treasure chests. Treasure chests! You've found the treasure!

But...maybe you should peek inside one of the chests before you wake Long John. You tiptoe over to the biggest one. The lock is rusted away. Slowly you open it. Wow! The chest is full of gold!

Suddenly someone pushes you from behind. You topple into the chest. BAM! The lid slams shut.

"Hey!" you cry, pushing at the lid.

Mad Monty laughs and shouts, "Don't go away!"

Fat chance! Well, you've got enough gold to buy the world's best drum set. But if someone doesn't open the chest pretty soon, this is going to be...

THE END

You wave your arms! You point to your throat!

Finally, Gonzo notices. "Hey, cool," he says. "You're turning blue! Great color on you."

"Shiver me timbers!" cries Long John. He drops the bowl of eggs he's whisking and rushes to your side. He spins you around, places his fists directly over your abdomen, and gives a mighty thrust! The chicken bone flies out of your mouth.

You rub your throat. Boy, that was a close one!

"Th–thanks, Long John," you manage.

"Anytime," says the cook. "Bone in the throat is no problem, not for ol' Long John." Then he frowns. "But food poisoning..." He shakes his head. "Still have a problem knowing what to do about that."

"Food poisoning?" you ask, feeling very queasy.

"Aye," says Long John. "Happens all the time on these long sea voyages."

"But we haven't even left the dock yet!" you say. Now you're feeling *really* sick. "Where...where's the bathroom?" you moan.

"On a ship," says Jim, "the bathroom is called the head."

Whatever it's called, you're never gonna make it. Sorry, sailor! Looks like it's...

THE END

You open *Muppets Forever!* There's good old Fozzie, Gonzo, Kermit, and Miss Piggy. And on the next page, there's Rizzo and a bunch of his rat buddies. Boy, do you ever love those Muppets!

You start reading. You keep reading. Yep, it's as good a story as it ever was. You read all the way to...

THE END

Huh? you say. *What's this?* you say. *What kind of a cheap trick is this, anyway?* You think this ending is totally boring? That it can't really be...

THE END?

Oh, all right, all right. Go back to page 9. Read it over again. This time when you come to the choices, pick *Treasure Island*. But at the end of that story, if you die a horrible death at the hands of bloodthirsty pirates, don't blame me!

"That's the treasure map!" exclaims Jim.

"Oh, boy!" shouts Gonzo. "We're gonna be rich!"

"Yeah!" you agree. "And I'm going to buy myself the most amazing set of drums!"

"Whatever," says Rizzo. "Come on! We have to hire a ship to take us to Treasure Island!"

Two short days later, you're standing with Jim and Gonzo on the deck of the *Hispaniola*.

A horse–drawn coach stops beside the ship. "Make way for Captain Smollett!" shouts Mr. Arrow, the first mate. The coach door opens and out steps the captain.

"He looks a little green to me," says Gonzo.

Go to page 26.

"Pull up the gangplank!" shouts Mr. Arrow.

"I hope Rizzo's on board," says Gonzo, worried.

"There he is," says Jim, pointing to a narrow gangplank next to the main one.

Yep. It's Rizzo, all right. Plus dozens of other rats—all wearing Hawaiian shirts. They've got cameras slung around their necks, too.

"They gotta be tourists," Gonzo observes.

Rizzo is holding a tiny clipboard. As the tourist rats come aboard, he checks off their names.

The three of you walk over to see what's going on.

"Rizzo?" says Gonzo. "What *is* this?"

"Rat Tours, Limited." Rizzo grins. "I figured I might as well make a few bucks while I'm here." Then he whistles to a young rat couple who are smooching by the rail. "Randy! Donna!" he calls. "Honeymooners! Yo!"

When they stroll over, Rizzo turns to you. "Show Mr. and Mrs. Plagueman to their cabin, will you? It's the rat hole behind the grease can in the galley."

Is hanging out with lovesick rats what you want to do right now? Or would you rather stay on deck?

Can't decide? Flip a coin!
Heads: **You do Rizzo the favor.**
Go on to the next page.

Tails: **Point the Plaguemans toward the galley.**
Don't worry. They'll find it.
Then turn to page 38.

You lead the Plaguemans to their hole...er, cabin. Randy pops in to check the room.

"Well, enjoy the trip," you tell Mrs. Plagueman.

"Wait a sec," squeaks Donna. "I know Randy has a tip for you. Randy? *Randy!*"

"That's okay," you say, backing away.

"I do if you can break a fifty," says Randy, emerging from the hole. "And, say, where's the snack bar? What's a rat gotta do to get a bite around here?"

You end up giving the Plaguemans a tour of the *Hispaniola*, from stem to stern to crow's nest. It takes all day. And...it's sort of fun. The Plaguemans seem very impressed. Randy never does break that fifty, but at the end of the day he gives you the whole thing! Hmmm, there's money to be made as a rat tour guide.

The next day, Randy and Donna recommend you to their friends, Milt and Shirley Verminelli. Talk about a "fun couple"! After that, you're booked solid for the rest of the trip. Rizzo offers to make you a full partner in Rat Tours, Ltd.

"It's a deal," you say. You and Rizzo shake on it.

You're sorry when this voyage comes to...

THE END

You back up ever so slowly, not making a sound. Step by step, you back deeper into the jungle. You don't turn around. So you don't see that you are backing right into...

"Whoa!" you cry. A pair of arms grabs you. They savagely spin you around. You're face–to–face with a big, burly wild boar!

Go to page 29.

But it's not just one boar—it's *five* of them! They've got bones in their noses. They've got on skull necklaces. Their spears are pointing right at you!

The boars start grunting and snorting up a storm. Suddenly one of the boars scoops you up. He throws you over his shoulder, holding you by the back of your knees. You're getting up your nerve to mention that it's really, *really* uncomfortable being held upside down this way, when the boars start running.

Off they trot, deeper into the jungle. Talk about a bumpy ride! Your head is bouncing around on the back of that boar like a basketball at an NBA playoff game. You're not all that sorry when you pass out.

You wake up. The *good* news is that you're no longer being carried off by a wild boar. Now you're in a clearing lit by flaming torches. The *bad* news is that you're tied to a post facing a stone altar. On the altar is a primitive drawing of a strange, plump beast.

Go to page 30.

In front of you stands a big, potbellied boar wearing a wild feathered headdress. You figure him for the chief. "Howdy vous, stinky froggy man and friends," says the boar.

"*Froggy man?*" you mutter. "What's this guy talking about?"

"Uh, I think he means me," says a voice.

You turn. Hey, you're not the only hapless victim tied to a post. Three others are right beside you. And sure enough, one of them is definitely a frog.

Go to page 31.

"The name's Smollett," the frog tells you.

"R-r-rizzo here," whispers the very nervous rat tied to the next post.

"Gonzo," says the guy next to the rat. He's got a nose like a spigot. "We'll get out of here some—"

"Silence!" the boar butts in. "I am King of Boars! You have violated sacred island!"

"Oh, great!" moans Rizzo. "Now we're gonna be hideously sacrificed at a pagan altar!"

"No!" shouts the king. "First, we torture *vous*."

The boars around the king begin chanting: "BOOM SHA-KAL-A-KAL!" One strikes a gong and a primitive ceremony begins. Other boars start dancing, beating drums, waving spears. The chanting grows louder: "BOOM SHA-KAL-A-KAL!" Boar maidens dressed in white appear, flinging orchid petals. Behind them come warrior boars. And then an elephant! He's carrying a tent on his back.

The elephant stops. The tent flaps part and out steps a gorgeous lady pig. A jungle goddess!

The boars carry you and your buddies to the altar.

"Kneel!" shouts the king.

Yikes! Looks as if you're about to be sacrificed to the boar goddess!

If you think that's what it looks like, turn to page 5.

If you think there's still some chance that you can escape, turn to page 53.

Treasure Island it is. You open the old book again. But what's this? Somebody's written in it! Boy, if your school librarian, Ms. O'Connor, could see this, she'd go ballistic!

The handwriting is really wobbly. But you try to read what it says:

IF A SAILING SHIP YOU'D STEER,
IF STORM NOR SHARK NOR PIRATES FEAR,
IF BURIED GOLD YOU WISH TO SEEK,
THEN "PIECES OF EIGHT" YOUR TONGUE
    SHALL SPEAK.

If you say "Pieces of eight," turn to page 39.

If you say "Are you kidding?" and decide to get an early start on your math homework for Monday, turn to page 4.

Congratulations! You got it! These pirates are not too bright. So get busy and outsmart them!

"Look, guys," you say as you begin taking off your watch, your *last* year's birthday present.

The pirates look on suspiciously.

"This is a *watch*," you explain, dangling it by its strap. "With this, you can throw away all those clunky hourglasses. With this, you'll never be late for a plank-walking again!"

You step forward, holding out the watch to Long John. "Take it," you say. "It's yours. Check out the movement of those stars and comets!"

Long John takes the watch. He examines it.

Scowling, he hands it back to you. "This is a worthless bauble," he declares. "I see no movement."

You take the watch back. Long John's right. Nothing's happening! Your watch has stopped! You shake it. Nothing. Finally it dawns on you. That guaranteed–for–one–year battery! A year's up. It's dead.

And that's what you're going to be, too, unless you can think of something!

Think hard. Really hard!
Then turn to page 20.

Uh-oh. This does not look promising.

If you think you can wiggle out of this one, turn to page 56.

If you think you're done for, kaput, zapped, fried, shot, drawn and quartered, and, for all practical purposes, dead meat, turn to page 12.

"Not really," you tell him. "What I'd like to be is a drummer in a rock band."

"But wouldn't you like a chest full of gold?" Long John asks. "Gold enough to buy yourself the fanciest set of drums anyone ever laid eyes on?"

"Well, sure," you admit.

"That's the spirit!" Long John grins and pulls a map from the inside of his coat. "Read this for me."

As you look at it, the pirates gather around you.

"But why?" you ask. "Can't you read?"

"Of course we can!" growls a hairy little pirate with a weird top hat. "Hard words, too. Like *kill* and *die* and *murder* and *stab* and *fatally wounded...*"

"Enough, Mad Monty!" says Long John. He smiles at you. "We just want to see if *you* can read it."

You read: "*Take 620 giant steps south. Take 987 baby steps east. If you get out of line, go directly to Jail. Do not pass Go. Do not collect $200. When you see three skeletons hanging from a tree, you're there.*"

"Okay, let's go," you say. "Follow me, men!"

The pirates line up behind you. You start on the giant steps: "One, two, three, four, five, six..."

Go to page 21.

You don't move a muscle. The three passengers climb out of the boat. One of them is wearing an admiral's suit. He reminds you of Fozzie Bear. He seems to be talking to...his finger? Another one is short and fat and wears glasses. The third one looks...confused.

The good news is you know these bozos aren't pirates, smugglers, or cutthroats.

You stand up and yell, "Excuse me, sirs!"

"Oh, look!" says the admiral. "This island is inhabited!" He beckons you over. "I'd like you to meet Mr. Bimbo," he tells you. "He lives in my finger."

"Um, nice to meet you, Mr. Bimbo," you mumble.

"Such strange garb the native wears," says the short one. Is he talking about your sweatshirt?

Quickly, you explain how you got there. "And," you finish up, "there's a band of bloodthirsty pirates on the other side of the island!"

"Actually," says Long John, stepping out of the brush, "we're on *this* side of the island now."

The whole evil bunch steps onto the beach. They're drawing their swords. They're pointing their muskets.

"Good-bye, Mr. Bimbo," says the admiral.

He's a bozo, but at least he knows that it's...

THE END

You're on deck as the ship sails out of the harbor. Mr. Arrow starts the role call:

"Long John Silver!"

"Aye," answers Long John.

"Mad Monty!"

"Aye! Aye! Aye!" screams a truly deranged-looking seaman in a top hat. He thrusts a dagger in the air.

"Polly Lobster!"

"Aye! Gimme a cracker! Squawk!" cries a large lobster perched on Long John's shoulder.

"Weird," whispers Gonzo. "Very weird."

"Clueless Morgan!" calls Mr. Arrow.

"Huh?" says a big, not-too-bright sailor.

"Awk! Turn around, Clueless!" screams Polly.

"Huh?" says Clueless. He begins turning around and around and around.

What a crew! you think.

"You three," says Captain Smollett, striding up to Jim, Gonzo, and Rizzo. "Come to my cabin immediately."

You watch your friends follow the frog. Feeling left out, you stroll along the deck. You climb a spiral staircase. Then you stop short. You hear something. You're not alone on the upper deck!

Go to page 47.

"Huh?" you say. "*Pieces of eight?*"

Suddenly, the lights go out. Yikes! What's happening? It's pitch–dark. Your room starts spinning! Your bed starts bucking like a bronco! You feel like yelling, "Auntie Em! Uncle Henry! It's a twister!" But all you can do is grip the books on your lap for all you're worth.

Just when it seems that you can't take it any longer, the spinning stops. But...where are you?

Go to page 40.

You're sitting at a table in what seems to be a restaurant. But it's sure no McDonald's. Or even House of Pancakes.

This place is old. A fire's burning in a fireplace. The tables are full of strange people and...*creatures*. They're drinking from big mugs. They're dressed funny. Like they're in a play or something from about two hundred years ago. Then it hits you. It's the illustration from *Treasure Island*. And you're *in* it!

But you don't have time to think about this, because you notice that you aren't the only one at your table. There's also a really grisly, smelly old guy. Swiftly, he turns toward you. The flames from the fireplace reflect in his scary-looking eyes.

"Ol' Flint up and died," he growls.

"What?" you say.

"Died 'afore he could return to that cursed island and dig up his treasure," he adds in a raspy voice.

"Um...excuse me?" you say.

"Why?" a voice behind you asks. "Did you burp?"

You whirl around to see a rat. He's wearing a waiter's apron. And carrying a tray.

"The name's Rizzo," says the rat. "And I'll be your waiter tonight. So, what'll it be? More grog?"

Go to page 41.

"Rizzo?" you say.

"The one and only," he says, extending his little ratty paw for you to shake.

Wow, you think. You look down in your lap. The two books are still there. *I get the feeling there's been a mix-up*, you think as you see what looks like Gonzo walking toward your table. Hose nose. Three straggly feathers on top of his head. Yep, it's Gonzo.

Walking next to him is a boy. His clothes are sort of ragged. He looks about your age.

"Closing time," Gonzo says. "Say, is that your stomach growling?"

"I guess," you say, feeling embarrassed.

"Well, we could get you a steak-and-kidney pie," says Gonzo. "Or a nice mutton stew. Or maybe a freshly roasted free-range chicken—except for one thing."

"What's that?" you ask.

Go to page 42.

"The kitchen's closed," says Gonzo.

"Oh," you say. "Well, I didn't bring any money with me anyway."

Rizzo looks thoughtful. "Actually," he says, "we've got some table scraps."

"Yuck," you say.

"I hear you!" exclaims the rat. "All we ever eat are table scraps! I hate table scraps! I *hate* 'em!"

While Rizzo is ranting, the boy turns to you. "I'm Jim Hawkins," he says. "Come on. Maybe we can find something better than table scraps in the kitchen."

You, Rizzo, and Gonzo follow Jim. In the kitchen, dirty dishes are stacked to the ceiling.

You and Jim start going through the cabinets. But before you have time to find a snack, the kitchen door bursts open. In runs the old guy who was sitting at your table.

"Grog!" he cries. "I must have grog, lads!"

"Okay, Billy Bones," says Jim. "Just a small one."

"Grog 'til I float!" cries Billy. Then suddenly he grows quiet. "Listen!" he whispers. "You hear it?"

You listen. But all you can hear is a *tap, tap, tap*. The tapping grows louder and louder, and then...

Go to page 43.

BAM! BAM! BAM!

Someone's pounding on the kitchen door!

Terrified, Billy Bones throws his arms around your neck. Oh, man! Doesn't this Bones guy *ever* take a shower? P—ew! He stinks!

"Pew!" cries Billy. "It's Pew!"

"You can say that again," you mutter.

The door flies open. In walks a hideous scaled creature dressed in rags. He's got eye patches—over *both* eyes. And on each patch is a little skull and crossbones. Could it be? A real pirate!

"It's me, Blind Pew," says the pirate. "I know you're here, Bones. Come out, ye sniveling coward!"

Go to page 44.

You manage to unwrap Billy's arms from around your neck. Shaking with fear, he puts a finger to his lips. He's begging you not to tell Pew where he is.

Everyone stands in frozen silence while Pew bumbles about. As he crosses the room, you see that he's left the kitchen door open. Wide open! If you want out, here's your chance!

Go ahead—make a run for it!
Then turn to page 48.

Don't risk it! Stick around in the kitchen
and turn to page 16.

After a very bumpy coach ride, you all arrive at the harbor. You walk toward a most magnificent ship.

"There she is," says the squire. "The *Hispaniola!*"

"Wow!" says Jim Hawkins.

You have to admit, it is a pretty amazing ship. Except for the figurehead on the front. Make that figure*heads*. They look just like Statler and Waldorf, those two old guys from "The Muppet Show."

Suddenly Statler shouts, "Hey, *you!* What're you staring at, kid? Did you think figureheads were always beautiful, half-dressed young ladies?"

"Too bad if you did!" chimes in Waldorf.

The two old geezers crack up, laughing.

Go to page 46.

You follow Jim Hawkins, Gonzo, Rizzo, and the young squire on board. The crew is busy polishing brass, swabbing decks, and mending the rigging.

"Where's the kitchen?" says Rizzo. "I'm starved."

Come to think of it, so are you.

Jim leads the way down some narrow stairs. "On a ship," he says, "the kitchen is called the galley."

"I don't care what it's called," says Rizzo. "As long as it's got FOOD!"

"Food?" a face peers around the corner. It belongs to a tall man who's whisking eggs. He looks cheerful. But there's something about him you don't entirely trust. "Did I hear someone mention food?" he asks.

"That'd be me," says Rizzo.

"Well, you've come to the right place," says the man as he beckons you inside. Everywhere you look, you see roasted chickens and homemade pies. "I'm the ship's cook, Long John Silver. Go ahead, help yourself."

Rizzo dives for the nearest chicken. You snap off a wing and start gnawing. Mmmm! It's tasty! You're really digging in now. But—oh, no! A little bone! It's stuck in your throat! You're...you're choking!

If you think Long John Silver knows the Heimlich maneuver, turn to page 23.

If it occurs to you that Dr. Heimlich hasn't even been born yet, turn to page 49.

You duck behind a post and listen.

"Pew swore those kids had the treasure map," Polly Lobster says. He isn't talking like a parrot anymore.

"I say we kill 'em!" shouts Mad Monty. "Tear 'em to pieces! Cut out their livers! Kill! Kill! Kill!"

You peek out from behind the post. Monty's whipping his sword around his head. Swish! Swish! He slices the feathers right off Clueless Morgan's hat.

"Hey!" cries Clueless. "He killed my hat, Polly!"

"Pipe down, you ninnies!" growls Polly. "I say we grab the captain and run the ship ourselves!"

Wow! These guys are planning a mutiny! You've got to tell Captain Smollett!

You sneak out from behind the post. Quickly you tiptoe to the staircase. You're just about to dash down when you hear Polly's voice behind you: "Where do you think you're going, eh, mate?"

You whip your head around. Right behind you, Polly's glaring at you. Monty's sword is drawn. Clueless is trying to arrange what's left of the feathers on his hat.

Yikes! What are you going to do?

If you want to make a run for it, turn to page 52.

If you want to stick around and fight it out with Monty, turn to page 13, and good luck!

As Pew begins insulting the moosehead on the wall, you catch Jim Hawkins' eye. You tilt your head toward the door. He nods. He's with you. So are Gonzo and Rizzo. So's Billy.

One, two, three! You make a dash for it!

Ooomph! In your haste, you all try to push through the narrow doorway together. Big mistake! Now you're all stuck.

Pew wheels around. Quick as lightning, he's at the door. He grabs Jim by the arm.

"Oooh, a pretty little girl, is it?" Pew sneers. "Take me to Billy Bones, my pet!"

"There's no Billy Bones here," Jim says. "And I'm not a girl!"

"All right, Miss Snippy Pants!" cries Pew. He lets go of Jim. He grabs *your* arm. He squeezes—tight.

"Ow!" you cry. "That hurts!"

"It'll hurt worse every second you don't tell me where Bones is, you whimpering puppy!" growls Pew.

Oh, ow! Pew isn't kidding. You don't think you can stand it much longer. He's crushing *your* bones!

If you want to tell Pew where Billy is, turn to page 50.

If you want to grit your teeth and keep quiet, turn to page 11.

You fall to the floor. Just as the light starts to dim, Long John picks you up by your feet. He shakes you—hard! Ptooey! You spit out that bone.

"You're supposed to eat the *meat*," says Long John. "Not the bones!" Then he slaps you on the back. "Looks like I saved your life," he adds.

"Thanks," you whisper, which is all you can manage. That bone really messed up your throat.

Long John leans in close to you now. "Sailors have a tradition," he says. "A life saved is a life paid."

"Uh–oh," says Rizzo. "I think Long John just got himself an assistant."

"An assistant?" you say. "Well, sure. Okay."

Long John rubs his hands together. "All right, start by peeling those potatoes." He points to a huge mound of potatoes. They're stacked to the ceiling!

"Um...all of them?" you ask.

"Every one," says Long John. "Then mash them, make some gravy—not too fatty, mind you." As Long John speaks, he's untying his apron. He ties it on you. "Perfect fit!" he exclaims.

And so you start peeling. You never do get out of that kitchen, er, galley, until the voyage comes to...

THE END

"Here he is! Mr. Pew!" you squeal. "Here's the man you're after! Billy Bones!"

"What?" Pew drops your arm. "You're ratting on Billy?"

"I can't believe you did that," says Rizzo.

"Bad form," says Jim Hawkins.

Gonzo just looks away.

"But my arm!" you protest. "The pain—it was awful!" You look from Jim to Rizzo to Gonzo to Billy Bones to Pew. Disappointment is written on each face.

"Here," says Pew at last. He's holding something out to you.

"What's this?" you say, taking it. It's a scrap of paper, blank except for a black spot in the middle.

"It's the Black Spot," says Pew.

"I can see that," you say.

"It's the pirate death sentence," Pew whispers.

"Death sentence!" you cry. "But...but...but..."

"It were meant for Bones," Pew continues, "but after you gave Billy up like that..." He shakes his head.

Go to page 51.

Gonzo, Rizzo, Jim, Pew, and Bones are backing away from you now.

You start out the door. Then you stop. Right outside are a dozen ghastly pirates. Some have knives between their teeth. Others have cutlasses. Or pistols.

There's just one thing to do. Make a dash for it!

Out the door you run, taking the pirates by surprise. For a minute, they don't realize what's happening. By the time they do, you have a nice head start.

Keep running! That's the way. Don't look over your shoulder. It'll just slow you down. And you don't want that to happen. Because a couple of those pirates are gaining on you. Can you feel them breathing down your neck? And if they catch you, it's sure to be...

THE END

"Hey! Look out!" you cry, pointing to the sea.

Monty and Polly whip their heads around.

"Gotcha!" you yell. Then you zoom down the stairs. You race to Captain Smollett's cabin. You tell the Captain and Jim everything you heard.

Captain Smollett turns to Jim. "I must lock up the treasure map in my safe, lad," he says.

"Those pirates will know it's in your safe, Captain," says Jim. Then he turns and hands you the map. "But they'll never suspect that *you* have it."

Quickly, you stuff the map into your sweatshirt pocket. You walk out of Smollett's cabin whistling an innocent tune. No sign of pirates. You keep walking and whistling until you can't whistle another note. You sit down to rest in a deck chair and fall fast asleep.

When you wake up, it's dark. The map! Is it still in your pocket? You start to feel for it, but...you can't. Your hands are tied.

You're not in a deck chair anymore, either. You're in a jolly boat. In the moonlight, you see Mad Monty at the oars.

"Here we are!" Long John says as Monty lands the boat on Treasure Island.

Go to page 14.

"*Bonsoir, mes amis!*" the goddess says. "I am Benjamina Gunn." She surveys her subjects. When her eyes light on Captain Smollett, she gasps. "Untie the prisoners!" she cries. She rushes to the frog.

"Smolly?" she exclaims. "Can it be you?"

"Benjamina!" says Smollett.

Oh, joy! You're saved!

The goddess smiles sweetly. Then she doubles up her fist and smacks Smollett across the clearing.

"Tie 'em back on their stakes," orders Benjamina. "Then torch 'em!"

"Old girlfriend," Smollett explains as the boars carry you toward the fire. Sure looks like this is...

THE END

"Avast, Monty!" Long John yells. "Initiation's over. They're our pirate brothers!"

"Oh," says Monty. For a moment, he looks almost thoughtful. Then he brightens. "I've got a plan! Let's just kill this one! Arrrrgh!"

When Monty says "this one," he's talking about *you*! He sandwiches your neck between his cutlasses. Boy, are they sharp!

Long John takes his crutch and bats away Monty's swords. "Enough, you mad dog!" he roars.

Monty shrinks back. Then he lunges at Long John, who picks up a sword. The two of them start fighting.

You back away, rubbing the creases Monty left in your neck. Whew! That was a close one!

Now the other pirates are getting into the fight. They're swinging their cutlasses! They're firing their muskets! What a brawl!

Hey, maybe this would be the perfect time for you to slip away!

Go to page 55.

"Come on," you whisper to Jim.

He nods, and the two of you take off. You hurry toward the shore. You scurry past Dr. Teeth's band, which has just started playing another set.

"No offense," Zoot calls to you over the music, "but you guys don't exactly fit the pirate profile."

"We're not thieving pirates!" Jim says hotly.

"Pirates! Pirates!" chants Animal.

"Maybe they're, like, prisoners," suggests Floyd.

"Prisoners! Prisoners!" shouts Animal.

Boy, it's like an echo chamber around here!

"We're not prisoners!" declares Jim.

"I wouldn't be so sure," says Zoot.

"Really," says Floyd. "Like, look behind you."

Before you can look, Jim takes off again. He's leaping over the beach grass, flying into the jungle. He's out of there. He probably thinks you're right behind him. But you're not. You're still standing there, with your feet planted in the sand. Slowly, you turn and look behind you. Yikes!

What do you see? Quick!
Turn to pages 34–35 and find out!

You're kidding, right? Wriggle out of this one? No way!
Maybe you didn't get a really good *look* at those guys.
Maybe you'd better turn back to pages 34–35 and check
them out again. They're pirates, for heaven's sake. They
bring new meaning to the term *armed and dangerous!*
And all their arms are pointed at Y-O-U!

Your brain is spinning. Maybe if they think *you're*
armed, too, they won't shoot. Maybe if they think you
have a pistol, they'll back off.

Slowly, you slide your hand into the pocket of your
sweatshirt. You stick out your pointer finger. You sure
hope it looks like the muzzle of a...

Hey! *Ow!* Something *bit* you! You pull your hand out
of your pocket, and there's *Fluffy!* Your guinea pig is
hanging on to the end of your finger—by his teeth. Oh,
man! That hurts! You shake your hand. Fluffy loses his
grip. The furry little vampire falls to the sand. He
scurries away into the beach grass.

Which is more than you can do. You look up. The
pirates are advancing.

"Take aim!" cries Polly. "Fire!"

The last thing you see is a fiery blast. Yep, this is
definitely...

THE END